The Case of
the Man with the
Missing Forefinger

A story by

Allen Shoffner

authorHOUSE®

AuthorHouse™
1663 Liberty Drive
Bloomington, IN 47403
www.authorhouse.com
Phone: 1-800-839-8640

This is a work of fiction. All of the characters, names, incidents, organizations, and dialogue in this novel are either the products of the author's imagination or are used fictitiously.

Published by AuthorHouse 5/30/2013

ISBN: 978-1-4817-5708-9 (sc)
ISBN: 978-1-4817-5707-2 (e)

Library of Congress Control Number: 2013909506

Any people depicted in stock imagery provided by Thinkstock are models, and such images are being used for illustrative purposes only. Certain stock imagery © Thinkstock.

This book is printed on acid-free paper.

Introduction

The personal introduction of the author of a book is usually made by the publisher on the back cover. My introduction as an author can be found at page 71 which lists some of the publications I have previously authored.

As an attorney with more than fifty-six years of active trial and appellate practice in court rooms and the writing of legal documents, I have had the satisfaction of seeing much of what I have written published in briefs and law journals. I did this writing to make a living. Since my retirement as a practicing attorney, I have continued to write, not professionally as an attorney, but simply as an author, and I have had the satisfaction of seeing some of what I have written published in printed and bound books. I have done this writing for fun, or at least for its therapeutic value. I would like to introduce this latest work, *The Case of the Man With the Missing Forefinger.*

In some of my previous writing, the lead character tells the story in first person. Two stories of fiction included in my book, *Collectanea*, are examples of my work told and written in first person. This story is written in third person. It is different and unusual in another way. Most writers of fiction who have a story to tell start with a preconceived plot, and usually know before they start writing how the story begins and how it will end. To the contrary, I started writing this story not knowing where it would take me or how it would end. Instead of creating characters to fit a plot and story line, I have created characters that are writing this story for me and have taken me through the story from the beginning. When I completed Section 6 of this book, I realized that there was still a mystery which was unsolved, and I still did not know what the ending would be, which only the characters would provide.

The background and venue for this story is a fictional county in Tennessee. There are ninety-five counties in Tennessee, and many of them are located on rivers in the state. I have used a fictional name, Riverside County, for the name of the county in this story.

Readers may find errors in punctuation, spelling, and syntax, which have survived proof reading and spell checking. This is work of fiction, but the author is real. There is no ghostwriter. There is no pseudonym. I am solely responsible for its content. Mistakes or errors are mine, and mine alone.

Thank you for reading.

Allen Shoffner

Table of Contents

1

The Possum

"Possum, are you in there?"

The voice came from the driver of a car with bold lettering marked on each side and on the rear of the car: "The Sheriff of Riverside County." The car was parked with the motor running in a graveled driveway a few feet from the front door of a residence. The tone of the voice indicated that a prompt answer was expected. None was heard. The driver of the car emerged from the car. He was dressed in the uniform of a police officer and carried the usual gear of a police officer. His authority was exhibited on his badge: "Chief Deputy, Riverside County Sheriff." A passenger exited from the front seat of the car. The authority shown on his badge was "Deputy Sheriff, Riverside County." While standing by the opened door of the car, the Chief Deputy called out again:

"Hey, Possum, we need your help, we have another missing person case."

He was answered by a shrill voice which was easily heard from an open window of the building:

"What is the password?"

"Possum, tell that parrot to shut up and come on out."

1

Another voice within the house was heard, its syllables spoken in a drawl with a southern twang: "Ok, I'm coming."

A screen door screeched open and a man came out on the porch. He was dressed in denim bib overalls. He appeared to be middle age. He had a short beard flecked with gray hair. A Farmer Coop cap was tilted on the back of his head. That was Possum. Possum was not his birth name, but a name which came back with him from the war in Vietnam. He was addressed as Possum in the Sheriff's office because he had earned it in the war. The Sheriff was also impressed by his analytical and perceived magical and mystic powers and thought that "Possum" fit his personality. Possum was known as a psychic and a mentalist. He had a reputation among the public and even with some police departments as a mind reader, a clairvoyant, a solver of crimes, a finder of missing persons, and a fortune teller. Possum's real birth name was Isaiah Amos Maxwell, also known informally as just Max. Possum not only had two names, but he also had two personae: One persona was used in his private practice as a mentalist, telling fortunes and solving problems, both real and imagined, for individuals; and the other persona was used as a commissioned detective in the Sheriff's Department of Riverside County.

When Possum exercised his persona as a commissioned detective he used his more formal name, Detective Maxwell. He was unobtrusive. He did not visibly carry the typical hardware. His badge was carefully fixed on the inside of a belt. He was not furnished and did not drive a marked police car. When exercising his perceived powers as a psychic practitioner, Possum did not make claims which involved the practice of regulated professions and privileges. He did not claim that he could cure physical illness; he did not prescribe medicine; and he did not give legal advice, although his advice and services may have had more value to his clients than those performed by some practitioners in licensed and regulated professions. He did not give financial advice. He avoided seeing clients with domestic issues and people wanting advice about love and romance. They could consult the mind readers in the classified section of the Farmer's Almanac. He was not a soothsayer who predicted cosmic events like the end of the world. He focused on events which had already happened. And he never claimed to know where Jimmy Hoffa was buried.

Possum did not claim to be a magician, but he knew a few "tricks" and was frequently called upon to exercise his magic and reputed psychic powers by entertaining civic and professional groups. He entertained children at Halloween with unusual stories, such as reading minds and talking in séances with dead people. He did not use a crystal ball, astrology charts, or tarot cards. Most of his clients considered these aids "old technology."

Possum lived alone, unless one considered Pete a live-in companion. Pete was an African Grey Parrot. Pete could talk and used a graphic vocabulary. Possum lived on a country road in an isolated area of Riverside County. He did not have a barking dog, but he did have a talking bird which asked strangers for the password and provided Possum with an early warning system. Possum protected his privacy. He did not use e-mail, facebook, twitter, ipads, or other electronic devices. No name was on the mailbox.

Isaiah Amos Maxwell did not have a formal education. But he had been "educated" in the Vietnam War. As a young man he had gone to fight for his country. He came back an older man, disillusioned, to a country that did not appreciate the fight. The country lost the war and fifty-eight thousand of its best. Possum lost the best part of his life and came back with physical scars. He earned the Purple Heart. But he lost his wife who married another while he was away and took their two children with her.

Possum learned the hard way that in order to survive in the jungles of Vietnam he had to know where the enemy was hiding before they knew where he was. He had to know where they had laid the mines before he tripped the wires. Possum had grown up on a farm where he had learned from fishing and hunting how to identify and follow the tracks left by animals. And in the jungles of Vietnam he had to be alert for disturbed vegetation and tracks left by an enemy that wanted to kill him before he killed them. This also accounted for his interest in talking birds, such as Pete, which helped alert him to the presence of the enemy. On one occasion while on a search and destroy mission, which he did not like to talk about, the enemy ambushed his squad, killing all of the men, except Possum, who was thought to be dead too. But Possum lay on the ground in a crumpled death like fetal position, without moving, with blood draining from his chest, and the enemy moved on. Possum played possum and survived.

Possum brought this part of his persona to the Sheriff's office of Riverside County. He may have been considered eccentric by some. But he was not dumb. He just acted dumb. He was self educated in forensic psychology and had in his library *Studies In Criminal Psychology*, along with books on many other subjects. Possum acted like a possum and his reputation as a psychic did not depend upon any supernatural psychic ability but on instinct and his natural ability to listen, instead of talk, his concentration on details others had overlooked, and his common sense analysis of the results. His ability to act dumb was an advantage in detective work, especially when talking to experienced criminals who thought he was dumb. He understood that success in detective work, like playing poker, depended at times on what the accused thought the detective knew, not what the detective actually knew.

Possum used this psychology in such a way that on some occasions the person of interest or accused, when facing Possum, eye to eye, and fearful of Possum's presumed knowledge, would blurt out a confession or incriminating statement without even waiting for a Miranda.

Although some police departments occasionally used "consultations" with psychics in police work, this was never officially recognized because it tended to make the police, who had forensic science available for investigation, appear inept.

"Come on, Possum, let's go. Spit out your chewing tobacco and get in the car. You will be briefed about the missing person when we get back to town."

"Ok, let me put on my boots."

2

The Missing Person

"Come in men," invited Jim Drake, the Sheriff of Riverside County. Sheriff Drake was a typical country county sheriff. He did not usually dress in a uniform but dressed conservatively in civilian clothes. He wore a large Texas style Stetson hat on which he was careful to pin in plain view the badge of the chief law enforcement officer of Riverside County. He also carried a holstered gun in plain view on his belt. Sheriff Drake was an affable fellow who maintained friendly relationships with other politicians and community.

Detective Maxwell was escorted by the deputies into a room through a door lettered, "Sheriff's Office, Crime Busters of Riverside County, Authorized Entry Only." This was the headquarters or command center in which reports of pending investigations and missing persons were made, in addition to opinions and comments expressed about the weather, politics, sports, and mundane subjects. It appears the Sheriff had decided that if crime could not be stopped at least he would try to bust it. The Sheriff's deputies, detectives, and Josh Wilson, an attorney from the District Attorney General's Office were seated around a table.

"Men, I have a job I was elected to do. As you know, the sheriff's office is a constitutional office, and the Legislature has listed in the Code thirty-one jobs for me to do. I am giving you a job to do too. You know, you have been reading in the newspapers and seeing on television news about the latest missing person in our county. Some reporters are waiting outside now for some news. You know, the public expects this department to clean up meth labs and the drug trade with sniffing dogs, fight gangs, investigate homicides, rapes, burglaries, thefts, shoplifters, deal legally with illegal immigrants, handle complaints from the humane society about cats and dogs, and dodge bullets. And we are also expected to find missing persons."

The Sheriff paused to take a deep breath.

"You know, thousands of persons in this country disappear every day. Some just take a long one way walk away from problems. You know, some missing persons fake death and show up later. Some are teenagers running away or taken from home. Some are spouses or live-in mates running from abusers. Some show up alive, some show up dead. Some children show up in age progression pictures in the IRS income tax instructions. I feel sorry for those kids. They have lost their childhood-and likely their lives too."

The Sheriff paused to sip coffee.

Pulling a photograph out of a file, he continued:

"You know, our department has been building a file on Henry M. Cates. He has been missing from his home for three weeks. This is his picture. As I understand the law—our legal counsel can guide us on this—it is no crime just to be a missing person, unless a false report is filed. But we have to spend a lot of time trying to determine if that person is missing live or missing dead. If missing dead, we might have to solve a homicide, or determine if it was suicide.

"This gentleman and his wife, Clara, live in a nice home over on the river. Their three children are away in college. The

7

family has been active in the community. They have been active in social life at the country club. Mr. Cates plays golf—some professional. He is in the car dealership here in town with a partner, Travis Spears. Cates and Spears are involved in a law suit over dissolution of the partnership. Clara Cates is a homemaker, but she has worked part time in the business. The story on the street is that the family has recently experienced serious financial losses. The couple does not have a reputation for bloody domestic fights, but Clara Cates filed for a protection order about a year ago, which was later withdrawn. Some have called her a desperate housewife. She reported her husband's absence a week ago. He had been absent about two weeks before her report. I don't know why she waited so long. She does not know why he is missing and thought he might be away on a hunting or fishing trip, or in a golf tournament, but gives no reason why he would leave their home without first telling her.

"Well, men, that is a brief history. Do we have a homicide, a suicide, or just a missing person? We don't even have persons of interest--at least not yet. Who will volunteer for this job? You know, we retired our bloodhounds."

There was silence in the room, but all eyes were on Detective Maxwell, referred to sometimes as Deputy "Max" when on assignment and informally referred to sometimes by his alias, Possum.

Max responded with a drawl: "Yeah, I know, you want me to snoop around in the Cates's garbage. What do I do when she says that what's in their garbage is none of my business and slams the door in my face?"

"Well, you can tell her that you are just trying to find her husband. Whatever you do, don't call a news conference. If a reporter saw you bending over scratching around in the trash cans with your back end hanging out, a picture of such a graphic scene over the internet would make this office look like comic bumbling gum shoe cops of Riverside County."

"I'll try to avoid a scene, Chief. I will just be looking for the innocent looking little soft stuff."

"Good, Max, you know that sometimes innocent looking little soft stuff leads to big hard stuff. That janitor who noticed the little piece of tape across the lock of the door in the Watergate did not know that it would lead to the resignation of the President of the United States."

3

The Wife

"Hello, Mrs. Cates, this is Detective Maxwell, calling from the Sheriff's office. I have been assigned to help you find your husband. May I drive out to talk to you?"

"I have already told the Sheriff all I know. You will not find my husband here. He is not hiding in a closet or under the bed."

"I understand, mam, but we may be able to find him somewhere else."

"Oh, well, come on. I will turn off the alarm at the driveway entrance."

Max drove an unmarked car out to the Cates's home, through the gated entrance, up the driveway along a line of magnolia trees, paused at the front door, and announced his presence using the heavy iron knocker on the door.

The door opened. A lady appeared, dressed lightly in athletic tights like one might wear in a gym. She appeared to be athletically fit and her athletic wear matched her trimly sculptured physical features. Her dark brown hair was streaked with mid age gray and worn in a coiffured bun tied with a red ribbon. Max's attention was distracted from his official mission and he stood mute in the doorway.

"Mr. Maxwell, come in. I can't tell you where my husband is, but I can tell you about him."

"That will help."

"Well, we never got along as well as some people think. We have been married 25 years. I washed dirty diapers, took kids to school, survived getting our three children through teenage and into expensive colleges, worked in the home and in the business at the same time. And what do I get out of all of this? My husband thinks that I am supposed to do all of this for nothing. I think he even thinks that I have been having an affair with his partner at the business. The business started going down headed toward bankruptcy after I quit working in it. He probably blames me for that too. They are fighting over a split of the partnership assets. Our marriage started going down along with the business, and I am fighting now for a fair split of marital property."

"Mrs. Cates, I am sorry about your misfortunes. Does your husband have life insurance?"

"Yes, unless he quit paying the premiums."

"Who are the beneficiaries?"

"I am supposed to be beneficiary on one policy and his partner is beneficiary on another policy which is some kind of a business policy covering each other. He would have an interest in seeing that Henry stayed missing, wouldn't he?"

"The Sheriff's office has a record that you asked the Court for a protection order about a year ago, which you dismissed."

"That's right. He was threatening and knocking me around. I dropped it when he promised not to do it again.

"I should mention that Henry is an addicted high stakes gambler and carries a lot of cash around with him. He usually leaves more in Las Vegas than he brings home."

"Was your husband under medication?"

"He was taking medicine for high blood pressure but it was under control."

"When did you last see him."

"When I got up one morning, he was not in his bed. We slept in different beds. I looked in the garage and his car was still there. It would not have been unusual for one of his golf or fishing buddies to have come by and picked him up."

"Did he take his golf or fishing gear with him?"

"Well, to tell you the truth, I didn't look. I really didn't care where he was."

"Mrs. Cates, I would like to look around while I am here."

"You don't think that I had anything to do with his disappearance, do you."

"No, mam, no one has accused you and what I think does not matter."

"I will need to talk to my lawyer first."

Max was invited back out the door. He drove back down the driveway to the Sheriff's office. At least he could report that there was more than one person who had equal motives and equal opportunities to become persons of interest.

On his way back to the office Max weighed in his mind that Clara Cates had provided an impression and very little information. He realized that he would need to allow Spears equal time to talk about the Cates.

4

The Search

Max pulled his car up to the front of a building branded with a marquee sign, "CATES & SPEARS MOTORS". Branded pennants streamed in the parking lot, along with bouncing balloons. Before Max could exit his car he was greeted by a gentleman with "Cates & Spears Motors" imprinted on his jacket.

"May I help you?"

"Thanks for asking. I am not here to buy a car. I am Detective Maxwell from the Sheriff's office. I would like to talk to Mr. Spears about Mr. Cates missing."

"I will see if he is available."

After several minutes a gentleman, presumably Travis Spears. appeared.

"I understand that you are looking for Cates."

"Yes, sir."

"Well, I am looking for him too. If you find him, let me know. I have subpoenaed him for a deposition in a lawsuit. He is running from it. He is also running with financial records and money from our office. If I find him before you do, I am going to give him a fist whipping. His wife could give him a physical whipping too. She has been learning martial arts at the gym and she is capable of laying Henry out with a kick. They have been fighting in a bitter divorce case. She has several good reasons to get rid of Henry and different ways of doing it."

Max drawled: "It appears that the Cates have not been a very peaceful and loving family. The Sheriff tries to maintain law and order whenever he can. When did you last see Mr. Cates?"

"To tell you the truth, I don't remember. He was absent from the office for days at a time without offering any reason. He started gambling heavily, probably using company money to cover his losses. Henry hung out with a rough crowd. I realized that he was missing when I found that the company's records were missing. I understand that his wife reported his absence."

In order to keep the conversation going, Max said: "That's right."

"Mr. Maxwell, have you ruled out suicide? He could have decided to get in his boat in the Gulf and jump into a school of piranha."

Max replied in measured drawl: "There must be a better way to end it all. The Sheriff has not ruled out suicide, accidental death, homicide—he could have even died with a heart attack."

"Mr. Maxwell, Henry had many reasons to be missing."

5

The News Reporters

When Detective Maxwell arrived back at the crime control command center, he was greeted by the Sheriff who had a serious sphinx-like expression. Others in the room were snickering.

"What are you laughing about?"

"Max, I am not laughing," corrected the Sheriff. "But the news reporters and even some law enforcement people are laughing. Look at this cartoon, using my face as a comic character: 'The Sheriff of Riverside County sends a psychic sleuth out to investigate crime.' This story makes our department look like we get tangled up in our crime scene tape. They don't report that you are a thorough and professional investigator and that we use the latest forensic technology. But the media thinks that this story has entertainment value and they have sent it out on the internet wires, where it will be twittered, blogged, talked about on talk shows, maybe a story for Mad Magazine or even for the Wall Street Journal. I will be getting calls asking where you went to voodoo school. I can tell them that at least you did not get your training at Harvard or Yale. Forensic tests are not foolproof either and lab technicians have been known to mess up evidence. And the media reported several years ago that even Nancy Reagan consulted her astrologer occasionally."

"I haven't even made a report yet, Chief."

"Max, do you have any idea how they knew you were on the case?

"Nobody asked me. Mrs. Cates and Mr. Spears may have known that I did a little psychic work on the side."

"Max, when you do work for me, it is not on the side."

"I understand, Chief. Do you still think I should look thorough their garbage?"

"I will need to get a legal opinion from Josh about that. Josh, do we have to get a search warrant to look in a person's trash?"

"Sheriff, I will ask the Judge about that."

6

The Magistrate Judge

Judge John Sullivan was the magistrate judge of the Sessions Court of Riverside County. He was the judge who worked at the ground level of the judicial system. He presided over minor disputes between the citizens, tried minor misdemeanor charges, and issued search and arrest warrants. As a magistrate judge he acted as sort of a judicial gatekeeper at the courthouse. His office and court chambers were located in the courthouse. Judge Sullivan had been the senior practicing lawyer in Riverside County until he was elected magistrate judge. Judge Sullivan looked like a judge. He had a mangled mane of gray hair, matching gray eyebrows, and lines and wrinkles etched on his forehead. He used more frown wrinkles than smile wrinkles, especially when holding court.

Judge Sullivan was not only the magistrate judge exercising official duties, but unofficially he was usually available like an adjunct professor of law to help young lawyers with their continuing legal education by answering some of their legal questions.

Josh Wilson, the Assistant District Attorney, approached the Judge:

"Judge, I need to ask you about issuing a search warrant."

"Josh, what do you need a search warrant for?"

Josh explained the investigation made by Detective Maxwell, adding:

"And, Judge, Henry Cates has been missing another three weeks."

"Oh, yes, there has been a lot of talk at the coffee shop about the Cates. It sounds like they are in a messy, nasty divorce case. Now, Josh, you know that I can't issue a warrant based upon coffee shop talk."

"Well, Judge, Mrs. Cates and Mr. Spears have both made veiled threats and each has a motive."

"Josh, what do you want to search?"

"We want to send Detective Maxwell back out to search the Cates's garbage."

Judge Sullivan broke into a loud laugh, using some of his smile wrinkles.

"You want me to look ridiculous too? Come on, Josh, you don't have a body. You can't even tell me that a crime has been committed. You went to law school and read the Constitution, didn't you? Read it again. If I issued a search warrant, or if you sent your detective out there without a valid search warrant, Mrs. Cates would probably sue all of us.

Judge Sullivan proceeded with an adjunct lecture:

"You know that the Fourth Amendment was brought to this country from our mother country. You should know that there are only twenty-four words in the search and seizure clause of the Fourth, counting 'the' and 'and', and that there are only twenty-nine words in the warrant clause of the Fourth, counting 'the' and 'and.' You should remember that the Fourth has been enshrined in our Constitution since it was written, and has been applied to the states by the due process clause of the Fourteenth. You know that the Supremes have added many footnotes from time to time. You will find that the search and seizure clause of the Fourth protects the people from unreasonable search of their persons and houses.

"A person's person has been pretty well defined by the Supremes, but what does his house include? You need to research if a person's trash in a garbage can outside the house is protected. If it is part of that person's person or house, then it is probably protected from search without a search warrant unless the trash contains a body. You may find a case that a person has a reasonable expectation of privacy about his trash at least until it is taken to the landfill. Let me know if you find a body in it."

7

The Assistant District Attorney

The subject of missing persons, including Henry Cates, came back for discussion at the command center. The discussion was led by the state's lawyer, Josh Wilson:

"Gentlemen, the Judge gave me a lecture on constitutional law, but no search warrant. Before we can get a search warrant, we need a body, that is, a body that can be identified. Then, if there has been foul play, we need to identify the criminal. If we can't identify the criminal, the state will let us use a 'John Doe' warrant--I guess a 'Jane Doe' warrant would work too."

Sheriff Drake joined the discussion: "Then, Josh, as I understand the law, we can't do much about a missing person, as long as he or she remains missing?"

"Sheriff, that is about right."

"Josh, how long must a person be missing before he or she can be listed as a missing person?"

Josh gave a typical legal opinion: "Sheriff, that depends on the circumstances."

"Well, we have reported Cates missing to the FBI, the TBI, and registered him in the NCIC data base."

The discussion of missing persons then turned philosophical. That part of the discussion was led by the Sheriff:

"Do you fellows that how many persons disappear and are listed as missing every day in this country? Over two thousand three hundred a day! And most of the people they leave behind don't care. How can a person simply evaporate, or be atomized in a laser or some kind of cosmic event, or blow up in thin air, without leaving a trace, even for forensics?"

Josh answered: "It's been done before. It's the mysterious disappearance of famous persons that make the headlines. You know, Amelia Earhart disappeared without a trace somewhere in the ocean in 1937 and we have been looking for her for seventy-five years."

"Yes, I remember reading about the different theories for her disappearance. As I recall, her family hired a psychic to find her. She was not found alive, she was not found dead, but some remains and bones thought to be hers were found.

"And, Sheriff, it was reported on the news just recently that a jar of freckle cream thought to be Amelia's was found."

"Yes, I read about that too. And then there is D. B. Cooper, or the outlaw the FBI called D. B. Cooper, who hijacked the 727, stuffed $200,000 ransom money in his pockets, and jumped out in a parachute into the woods somewhere. The FBI is still looking for him. If thousands of experts with unlimited resources have not been able to find Amelia or D. B., our department should not get bad press if we can't find Henry Cates."

The Sheriff turned toward Max: "Max, what do we have on Cates?"

Max gave a short answer in a slow drawl: "Nothing but theories, Chief."

"OK, Max, what are your theories?"

Max gave the long answer in another measured drawl:

"Well, Clara Cates could have killed him; or she could have hired someone to kill him; or Spears could have killed him; or

Spears could have hired someone to kill him; or Cates could have faked his disappearance; or he could have killed himself; or he could have gone up in a helium balloon and forgot to turn off the gas and could be floating around in space somewhere."

"Well, Max, you will have to get out and find some facts to support the theories."

"That could be dangerous work, Chief. I will leave my funeral instructions at the front desk."

8

The Detective

"Hello, Mrs. Cates, this is Detective Maxwell calling from the Sheriff's office again. How are you today?"

"Not any better than I was yesterday."

"Has your husband come home yet?"

"This is not his home."

"I understand, mam, but I would like to finish my investigation out there. When I was there earlier, you said you wanted to talk to your lawyer."

"I don't need a lawyer. I haven't done a crime."

"Well, mam, maybe, you could help us find someone who has."

"Oh, well, come on, the gate is open, but watch out for my Doberman. He does not welcome strangers."

"Thank you, mam, I will be there in a few minutes."

Max drove through the gated entrance and up the gated driveway. Mrs. Cates and her Doberman met him at the front door. Max was a forensic psychologist, so in addition to looking for hard evidence in a trail which was growing cold, he would use unscientific methods in his investigation, such as interpreting body language and verbal clues which did not fit with the hard evidence and verbal statements.

"Mr. Maxwell, what are you looking for?"

"I'll just be looking, mam."

"What do you expect to find?"

"Answers to questions."

"Well, what are the questions?"

"Thank you, mam. Let's start with--what was your husband wearing when he left the house?"

"Now, Mr. Maxwell, for all I know he could have been wearing his pajamas. I told you that we slept in different beds and he was not in his bed when I got up."

"Did he leave his billfold?"

"Oh, no, he would not want me to look through his billfold."

"Did he leave his keys in the house?"

"No, he would not have wanted me to have them either. I do not know what he had keys for except his BMW and the little pick-up truck. He may have left in the pick-up because it was not in the garage when I looked out there."

"I guess he didn't take his toothbrush with him. Did he have a beard?"

"He was growing one—he was really fussy about that. He was growing and grooming a mustache and beard into what he thought was a distinctive artistic design."

"Do you have a picture?"

"I will try to find one."

"Mrs. Cates, mam, do you mind if I look around?"

"Well, I still don't know what you are looking for. You can look in his bedroom, computer room, bath, car, garage, but that is all. Everything else here is off limits. I may need a lawyer after all."

"I understand, mam."

Mrs. Cates followed Max closely as he moved slowly around

the area that she allowed. Max did not have a camera, tape recorder, magnifier glass, or any forensic kits, but he did have a pencil, and small shirt pocket note pad on which he scribbled some notes, and a photographic memory on which every detail was recorded. This kind of evidence may not have been worth much in court, but at least it was worth reporting to the command center.

Max sensed that anger and hostility simmered under Clara Cates' calm, controlled, and cosmetic surface appearance. It was time for him to leave.

"Mrs. Cates, call me any time. I can be reached anytime, 24/7."

9

The Trail

Max reported to the Sheriff and Josh at the command center:

"Chief, I have a few notes for you."

"Max, your note pad looks frayed. You know, the county commission keeps our department on a tight budget to avoid raising taxes, but we should be able to afford you a new note pad. What have you found this time?"

"The short answer is not much."

"OK, Max, I will listen to the long answer."

"Well, I looked around but only where Clara Cates allowed me to look. Mr. Cates's bedroom was left in a mess—clothes were scattered around the room—the bed covers remained unmade-- twisted in knots--which shows that he might have slept in knots too. Several bottles of vitamins were in the bath cabinet, along with what appeared to be sleeping pills and medicine for high blood pressure. Clara allowed me look through his computer room but not through what was on his computer."

"Max, that was a waste of time."

"That's right, Chief, but I noticed on a table by the computer some tickets for free slots at the Lucky Strike a casino in Tunica."

"That's interesting, Max, I'm glad you got the name because there several casinos in Tunica."

"I went out to the garage next where Mr. Cates's BMW was parked. I was able to look in the windows without Clara looking over my shoulder."

"What did you see there, Max?"

"I saw what looked like some business records in a banker's box in the floor of the back seat. There was a personal check book on the front seat—Riverside Bank."

"That's interesting too, Max. I am sure that his business partner would be interested in it, but it's not very useful for us."

Josh agreed: "If these items were in full view, a search warrant might not be needed, but we still do not have evidence that a crime has been committed."

"And, Chief, I forgot to tell you that I saw Henry Cates's golf bag in the back seat of the car and his fishing gear was in the garage."

"Well, fellows, we don't have any more than what we started with: Only individuals of interest who had motives and opportunities to account for Henry Cates' disappearance."

Josh added: "If motives were rated on a scale of one to ten, Clara Cates would probably rate a ten."

The Sheriff agreed: "That's about right for the financial motives, with some revenge added to the mix. And she had opportunities. You know, some spouses get a divorce with a butcher knife, a pretty nasty method that usually leaves a lot of blood. Others sometimes use cleaner methods like choking and strangling, putting rat poison in the coffee, and other ingenious methods."

Josh opined: "If Mrs. Cates used a non-traditional method to get a divorce she could not inherit or benefit from Henry Cates if convicted for murder. The state has what is called the slayer statute."

"Josh, that would be justice."

The Sheriff turned toward Max: "Max, it seems that Henry Cates has been spending time and money at the Lucky Strike casino. Get over there--you may be able to pick up his trail."

10

The Casino

Detective Maxwell had heard of the Tunica Resorts and the casinos which had become a modern gambling mecca in cotton fields on the Mississippi River. He understood that there were at least nine casinos operating there, attracting thousands of tourists, visitors, professional gamblers, and others operating outside or on the edge of the law. He had never been there, but he had a map. He would take a leisurely drive down U. S. Route 61. And on his drive down he would take time to think and talk to himself:

"Why am I on this chase to find a person who may not want to be found? Henry Cates could simply disappear anonymously into the crowds. The casinos and resorts even advertise and offer the 'opportunity to disappear.' The odds of finding Henry Cates are no better than my odds of winning the slots. And will my deputy's commission be good in Mississippi? I may be just another tourist. Josh Wilson didn't tell me if I had immunity in Mississippi. Oh, well, I could include a little entertainment on my expense account. I'll look for the Lucky Strike casino."

Max cruised through Tunica Resorts until he found a multi-story building with the marquee, "Lucky Strike Casino and

Hotel." He parked, entered the lobby, and asked to see the casino manager. In a few minutes, a gentleman appeared, with name and title on his jacket, "John Foster, Manager, Lucky Strike Casino." Max handed the manager his card and introduced himself:

"I am Detective Maxwell and I am looking for a missing person named Henry Cates. I have reason to believe that he is one of your patrons. I would appreciate your help."

"Mr. Maxwell, we have thousands of patrons here every day and every night. As you can see, there are hundreds here now as we speak, playing and having a good time. Most of our patrons are law abiding people who avoid publicity, and in order to provide them with the privacy which they expect we assign each patron a number. Everything done here is done in numbers. We know when a patron is playing, what games he is playing, and how much he wins or loses. Of course this allows us to reward complimentary items such free slot tickets to those patrons who bring us repeat business. We encourage all of our patrons to play responsibly, to drink responsibly, and to drive responsibly when they leave here, so they will come back. We don't want them playing on the grocery money, or with company money, or bet on the farm. I'm sorry but the casino rules don't allow me tell you if we have a Mr. Henry Cates on our list of patrons."

"I understand. This is his picture. He may have grown a mustache and beard after this picture was made. Do you mind if I look around while I am here?"

"Mr. Maxwell, don't you think you would look comical roaming around in our casino tapping our patrons on the shoulder to see if they look like Henry Cates?"

"They might think I was part of the floor show."

"Wait a minute, let me look closer at that picture--I have seen this fellow in our casino! He usually wears a jacket with Cates & Spears Motors on it, like the one in the picture. We have observed him from our one-way glass mirror over the gambling tables. He plays all of our games—craps, roulette, baccarat, blackjack, video poker—and he usually bring in to the table a stake with three or more zeroes. I see him here nearly every day. He may be staying in the casino hotel."

"Thanks for the lead."

"Mr. Maxwell, I have told you more than I should, but you seem to be a trustworthy fellow doing your job and there is something else you should know. Our security team is concerned that our patron, Cates, is usually with a fellow who has been barred from playing at our casino. This man is a felon out on parole from felony convictions, including some for violation of gambling laws. We suspect that our patron is gambling with this stranger's money. If he is, the stranger would be interested in protecting his investment by being sure that Cates kept the right books."

"That seems to be a logical assumption."

"Mr. Maxwell, I am sure you know there is a massive flow of money from racketeering and the underworld dark side of illegal gambling. They put illegal money into fronts that appear legal. They use proxies to carry the money bag. The racketeers follow the money. They not only follow the money--some will kill for it. Cates could be at risk."

"I hope he understands the risk."

"And, Mr. Maxwell, one other thing--the fellow following Cates is easily identified by an unusual physical mark: The forefinger on his right hand is missing. This would be his trigger finger if he is right handed."

11

The Report

Detective Maxwell talked to himself again on his way back to the command center. He was not able to bring Henry Cates back with him to the Sheriff of Riverside County. But he was able to bring back a mysterious note on his little scratch pad. At least he could tell the Sheriff where Henry Cates might be found.

"Congratulations, Max! I will call Mrs. Cates and tell her we found her husband at the Lucky Strike Casino."

"It won't be lucky for him, Chief."

"And I will need to tell the state's missing citizen alert bureau to remove his name from the missing persons list. You know, we had listed Cates as a missing citizen. That program is designed for old folks and people who have an impaired mental condition. Cates may have an impaired mental condition when Clara gets through with him."

Max nodded his head in agreement.

"You remember, Max, Clara got an order to protect her from Henry. Now, he may need an order to protect himself from Clara."

Max nodded his head again.

"Oh, well, maybe they could get on a TV reality show for help with their domestic problems. You know, Max, some movie stars, politicians, and other famous men can knock their wives around, come out for a press interview with their wives dabbling tears, apologize, and go on to the next crises as if nothing had happened."

"I know, Chief."

"And there is an ugly trend now toward ending marital problems with murder. I don't know if more wives are killing husbands or if more husbands are killing wives. But it is becoming a common alternative method of getting a divorce. It may not be cheaper, but it is quicker."

Max drawled: "It looks that way, Chief."

"Spouses used to murder their spouses by poisoning drink or food with hemlock, strychnine, arsenic, or some other lethal potion. Now, they hire it done. They don't have to bother with the details like cleaning up the job."

"And they still leave a job for us."

"That's right, Max, these professional contract killers are not on the internet; they may not even be listed on the crime network, but they are well known in the criminal underworld."

Josh added his comment to show his knowledge of classical history: "And she could have fed him poisoned mushrooms like Agrippina fed Claudius."

Max remembered that the check book lying on the front seat of the BMW appeared to be the personal check book of a joint checking account with Mrs. Cates.

"I can walk over to the Riverside Bank and find out if Clara has recently withdrawn more than grocery money out of this account."

"Well, you can try it, but I doubt that you will be furnished this information without a court order."

"I will talk to Miss Bessie. I think she trusts me."

12

The $5,000

Detective Maxwell opened the conversation with a measured drawl:

"Bessie, I need to talk to you privately."

Bessie invited Max to step from the cashier's window. "What do you need to talk about, Max?"

"Well, Bessie, you know that when I am not telling fortunes I am usually on an assignment for the Sheriff."

Bessie replied with a smile, "Yes, I know, Max, I want you to tell my fortune sometime." She paused and asked: "Are you here on some official business this morning?"

"Yes, mam. It involves one of your customers."

"Now, Max, you know that I can't give you financial information on our customer without the customer's agreement."

"Yes, mam, but I am on official police business."

"Who is the customer and what do you need to know?"

Max drawled slowly through a long answer: "Clara Cates--we have reasonable reason to believe she may have recently made a substantial withdrawal from her and her husband's joint checking account for an illegal purpose."

"Max, you know that banks are required to follow more regulations than there are books in the Library of Congress; we have to file more forms and reports than there are letters and numbers in the dictionary to give them. We have to file a CTR to make a Currency Transaction Report; we have to file a SAR to make a Suspicious Activity Report."

"Yes, mam, I understand."

"Wait here a minute, Max, I will look."

Bessie took slightly longer than a minute to look: "Max, our computer shows that Clara Cates withdrew $5,000 from the joint checking account two weeks ago. It was withdrawn in cash."

"Thanks, Bessie."

"And, Max, you are in luck. We will not have to file a CTR or a SAR report since the withdrawal was less than $10,000."

"Thanks, again, Bessie. Come on out sometime. I will consult with my astrologer, look in my tea leaves, and be sure that you have a good fortune."

Max mused on his way back to the command center: "Poor Henry. If Clara finances his murder out of their joint money, it would seem to be a rather inequitable division of marital property."

13

The Surveillance

Judge Sullivan addressed Josh Wilson, the state's Assistant Attorney General. Detective Maxwell listened.

"So, you think that you are ready now for a warrant to put a wire tap on Mrs. Cates. Josh, your updated explanation of the investigation shows that the Sheriff's office has been working hard on this case, but you need to be aware of how difficult it is to get convicting evidence, or even convincing evidence, through a wire tap. By the time law enforcement officers have learned how to use the latest technology in electronic surveillance, the underworld criminals have learned ways to avoid it. They don't have to use some sophisticated form of encryption. They have learned to follow the simple rule: NEVER talk on a wired telephone; NEVER use e-mail, and NEVER use cell phones, facebook, or twitter.

"Judge, that seems to be basic policy."

"However, our top spy, the four star general at the CIA, and his lover did not follow this simple rule. They thought they had a fool proof system worked out to carry on their secret affair: They set up an e-mail account under a fake name; each had the password to the account; each would write an e-mail to

36

the other, but instead of punching the send button they would simply use the draft folder as an electronic drop box."

"I followed the news about that, Judge. All of that would make best selling fiction if it were not true."

"It is stranger than fiction. It is weird. This is something that could be conceived only in Hollywood or our nation's capitol. But their dumb trick did not work. Somebody will probably write a book about it. Well, let me get to your request for a wire tap warrant. I have done some research of my own. The law in this state is clear that only a judge of competent jurisdiction may consider an application for wire tap or electronic surveillance. I hope that I am a competent judge, but I am only a magistrate judge. My court is not a court of competent jurisdiction because it is not a court of record. I am sorry, gentlemen, but this means that you will have to make your application to Judge Bacon, the Circuit Judge."

Josh thanked Judge Sullivan for another adjunct lesson in the law.

As they were leaving Judge Sullivan, Josh turned toward Max:

"Max, we can talk to the General, but we may be too late to save Henry Cates."

Max nodded.

14

The District Attorney General

District Attorneys General in Tennessee are elected every eight years to represent the State of Tennessee in their respective judicial districts. Some get their start in the criminal justice system by knowing the Governor and receiving a mid-term appointment. Many graduate through the criminal justice system from District Attorney General to Circuit Judge. John Calhoun was the District Attorney General in Riverside County. He assigned most trial work in Circuit Court to his assistant District Attorneys. John Calhoun had been elected and reelected District Attorney General. He was usually referred to as the "General."

The General opened the conversation, addressing Josh, his assistant, and Max, the chief deputy detective of Riverside County:

"Gentlemen, I understand that you want me to approve an application for a search warrant. I hope you understand the heavy responsibility of this office in complying with the constitutional, procedural, and technical requirements of search warrants. You can bet that smart defense lawyers understand the requirements. Of course, as you know, the purpose of these requirements is to balance the right of citizens to be protected from unlawful searches with their right to be protected from crime. But as you also know, the criminals are ahead of the prosecutors."

General Calhoun paused: "What do you want to search?"

Josh explained: "General, the Sheriff has credible information that a woman by the name of Clara Cates is planning to kill her husband. She has withdrawn $5,000 from a bank account which we believe will be used for a cash and carry contract job. A warrant is needed for a wire tap or a cell phone intercept and a GPS fix on her car."

"Josh, that's a pretty serious charge. Our wiretapping and electronic surveillance law is pretty serious too. You know the law: It is allowed only under compelling circumstances, only when authorized by a court of competent jurisdiction, and only upon a finding of probable cause. As you know, the statute covers every electronic device now known or imagined, except hearing aids. That sets the gate at a pretty high level. The statute also discourages surveillance which is dangerous for the law enforcement officer."

The General paused again and continued: "How do you propose to put a GPS on the woman's car? Trespassing to put it on would not be smart, and you might get shot doing it. And even if you were able to put on the GPS without getting shot and track her movements, our office would be embarrassed and look dumb if the device showed that she only went to the grocery store or out to get her hair done. And she could have withdrawn the $5,000 as part of her marital assets before her husband spent it."

The General continued with his analysis: "OK, consider a wire tap or intercept of e-mail—you know before you start that educated criminals never use a wired telephone or e-mail to plan crime. And every lawyer practicing criminal law in this country knows about the Supreme Court opinion in United

States v Jones, decided last year —actually the Supremes wrote three opinions, the majority opinion by Scalia, a concurring opinion by Sotomayor, and another concurring opinion by Alito. Josh, you know the story: The government stuck a GPS on the defendant's Jeep without a warrant and followed his movement from a central location. The Supremes held that this constituted an unlawful search under the Fourth. Defense lawyers will be making a lot of motions to suppress. I doubt that Judge Bacon would approve our application for a search warrant. Look, fellows, let's not look foolish, forget the electronics."

"Thanks, General, we still have Max here. We can dress him in a trench coat, a crazy hat, and send him out with a chew of tobacco. He can act like a possum, and do eyeball surveillance. He might even be able to draw upon his psychic powers."

Max listened in silence. He did not want to look foolish or be victim of crime.

15

The Dying Declaration

The dispatcher at the command center turned toward the Sheriff:

"Sheriff, we just got a call from the hospital--a man has collapsed in the emergency room who they think is Henry Cates. He was bleeding out from a deep stab wound. The emergency room doctor and nurses are trying to keep his vitals going. There may have been foul play."

The Sheriff turned toward Max: "Max, don't lose any time getting over there. Use my car, or the Chief Deputy's—turn on the siren and lights."

Max, the possum, did not usually do anything fast like talking fast or speed driving the Sheriff's police car, but this was an unusual assignment. The town's traffic moved over for Max on his way to the hospital. He turned into the emergency entrance. Max introduced himself as Detective Maxwell. He was met in the emergency room by the charge nurse, identified on her pin as Lois Wells, RN. Ms. Wells provided the interim history:

"This gentleman pulled himself into our emergency room, bleeding profusely from a deep stab into the heart. We don't know how he reached the hospital but he collapsed on the floor before we could even get him on the table. He could have been brought in and dumped at our front door, or he could have struggled to bring himself in. He is in shock—and he is not responding. I think we are losing him. We don't have any identification, but he may be the missing person you have been looking for."

"Yes, mam, that is Henry Cates."

Detective Maxwell was standing at the foot of the bed, and the triage nurses were at the side, when Henry Cates roused, trying to speak:

"I was robbed by a professional gambler." Henry Cates paused and struggled to continue, speaking slowly: "He thought I had money I had won at Tunica......." "He stabbed me......." "He left me to die........." "I don't know his name........., but the forefinger on his right hand is missing........."

Henry Cates then turned toward Ms. Wells. "Please tell my kids.............." His voice faded into an unintellible whisper as he struggled to continue and then stopped, leaving his last words unspoken in his last breath.

The monitor screens blinked blank and the nurses pulled a sheet over the face of Henry M. Cates.

"Ms. Wells, I am sorry you lost your patient. Thanks for calling us. The District Attorney may order an autopsy and want to take a statement. Will you include Mr. Cates's dying words in your medical records?"

"Yes, that would be a part of his medical history."

16

The Missing Man with the Missing Forefinger

The General, Josh, and Max sat down for a review. The General led the discussion. Josh and Max listened.

"Well, men, when we started this investigation we didn't have a body, we had no witness, no crime, not even persons of interest--just hunches and theories. Now, we have a body, a witness, a crime, and a missing criminal with the missing forefinger on his right hand. But we still do not have the name of the missing criminal that goes with the hand with the missing forefinger."

Josh queried: "General, how many criminals do you think are out there with the forefinger of the right hand missing?"

"Not many. That's an interesting question, Josh. You know, some organizations require secret rituals for membership, and secret signs, signals, tattoos, and handshakes to prove membership and loyalty to the organization. We see this happening in gangs and organized crime. Some in organized crime have even set up their own system of justice with rather severe penalties for those members who fail to follow the underworld code, like cutting off hands or fingers and leaving permanent scars. If this missing criminal was right handed he lost his trigger finger which may have been considered an appropriate penalty for someone who had shot someone in the underworld network."

"General, how do we get the name of this person?"

"Josh, that's another good question. We can try the NCIC data base. As you know, this is for individuals who have been fingerprinted and whose criminal record has been obtained, but we don't have fingerprints and we don't have a criminal record because we don't have a name to plug in. We don't have a social security number, or a driver's license number. The NCIC does have a file for unidentified persons, but we don't even have enough identifying information for that file, like age, race, height and weight, eye and hair color. The only identifying information we have now for this missing criminal is male sex and a missing forefinger."

Max offered encouragement: "This fellow may run, but he can't hide. He will show up somewhere, sometime, in a police lineup or morgue."

"Max, thanks for your work and support in this case. I doubt that this missing criminal will show up at my office and confess, but we will be ready when he is found. We will be prepared on the issues which will be raised by defense counsel. Josh, you can prepare a legal memorandum on the admissibility of the victim's dying declaration."

"General, that sounds like an assignment for the law review."

17

The Legal Research

J osh approached the General with a yellow legal pad and a handful of paper notes. "What do you have for me, Josh?"

"I have read the federal court cases, including those of the Supreme Court, the Tennessee cases, cases from other jurisdictions, and some articles in law reviews and law journals. I have research notes in this file. I can write a brief whenever we need to."

"Well, you can depend on the need for a brief. I expect a pretrial motion will be filed to suppress the dying declaration on multiple grounds. What have you found on the constitutional issue?"

Josh thumbed through his notes: "General, as you know, the Sixth Amendment to the Constitution of the United States is short and simple: It reads: 'In all criminal prosecutions, the accused shall enjoy the right to be confronted with the witnesses against him.'"

"Yes, I remember--that is what is known as the confrontation clause; and, as I recall, that's expressed a little differently in our State Constitution."

"That's correct, General." Josh picked up another note. "That is found in Article 1, Section 9. It says that in all prosecutions, the accused 'hath the right to meet witnesses face to face.'"

"Well, Josh, our missing accused may have been confronted by our deceased victim before he was stabbed, but it is too late for them to meet face to face in court. Have you found a way to get the dying declaration into evidence at trial?"

"I have, General. I have researched this from A to Z. It can be admitted under Rule 804(b)(2) of the Tennessee Rules of Evidence, and the long established common law of evidence admitting a dying declaration into evidence as an exception to the hearsay rule. The courts have listed five elements which must be shown before a dying declaration is admitted into evidence."

"What are they, Josh?"

"The first is that the declarant--that would be Henry Cates—is dead at the time of trial. We don't have a problem with that one.

The second is that the dying declaration is admissible only in a prosecution for criminal homicide. We should not have a problem with that one.

The third is that the declarant, Henry Cates, must be the victim of the homicide--no problem there.

The fourth is that the statement must be relevant to the cause or circumstances of the death.

And the fifth is that the declarant, Henry Cates, made the statement under the belief that his death was imminent.

We need to analyze items four and five."

"Josh, good work. As I recall my law school courses and Bar exam on criminal law and evidence, which includes a little Latin, dying declarations have been admitted *articulo mortis* on the theory that the awareness of impending death is as good as an oath. Why would anyone lie when taking his final breath on his death bed?"

"And General, we have a disinterested witness, the nurse at

the emergency room, who can testify that Henry Cates knew he was dying and wanted his children to know before he died that he had set up a trust for them. That is sort like a nuncupative will. And, in my opinion, his description of the circumstances of the attack and his description of his attacker eliminates Clara Cates as a suspect."

"Yes, I agree. Even if Mrs. Cates had formed an intent or conspired to hire a contract killer to kill her husband, there would probably not be a crime for which we could prosecute unless steps were taken to carry out the crime."

Josh added: "She ought to feel guilty."

Max drawled: "She ought to feel lucky."

18

The Call

The crimebusters at the Sheriff's Office of Riverside County had no time for rest. Calls to and from the dispatcher continued around the clock. It seemed that most criminals were out at night and that most crime was done under the cover of darkness. The crimebusters had little time to respond to the calls and less than little time for discussion of the calls. The lines to and from the NCIC had to be kept open 24/7. Occasionally the Sheriff was able to sit down with his deputies and staff for discussion:

"Fellows, you know we are expected to respond to these calls, even the stupid calls. We are called upon to help get drunk drivers off the road, pull their cars out of wrecks and ditches, settle domestic arguments, clean up meth labs, help take care of abandoned children, drag the rivers for victims of foul play, get cats out of trees, pick up dogs, and enforce all of the other laws on the books. Some of you are SROs assigned to protect our schools. We have to provide constitutional due process to the guilty, including free bed and board and free medical treatment for self-inflicted injuries. We get sued and you put your lives on the line in danger for the work you do. And for all of this you are overworked and under paid."

Heads around the room nodded in agreement.

"And men, there is another serious subject under recent discussion: Guns. Some people and groups are better armed than law enforcement. There are some crazy copy cat nuts out there killing people with military guns made for the purpose of killing people. And there are other nuts who think that we don't need to control these guns. These are not guns that we hang over our mantel and take with us to hunt deer, turkey, and behind our bird dogs to hunt quail and game to eat. These guns are used to kill police officers. This country has already lost control over the manufacture and sale of these weapons. Trying to recover them now would be like trying to put tooth paste back into the tube.

"And, there is more bad news. Some people and groups have been buying and hoarding ammunition causing a shortage of bullets for our own guns. There are enough guns and bullets out there to fight a war. I understand that when the Second Amendment was put in our Constitution to protect us from the British the musket was the main weapon, the sniper was the main shooter, and the Red Coat was the main target. Each shot had to count. The sniper had only about two minutes to pour the powder in, put the lead bullet on top of the powder, pack it all down with the rod, and in the meantime hope that he has not been hoisted on a British sword.

"Be sure to put on your armor and have a backup when you go out on calls."

"We will try to be prepared when we get them."

They did not have to wait long.

Nell, the dispatcher, addressed the Sheriff: "Chief, we just got a call from the Kentucky State Police. They are holding a male with the forefinger missing on his right hand."

"OK, tell them to hold him until we get there."

"Well, he won't hard to hold. He is dead. The patrol officer found him in a car which had run off the road near Paducah. They think that he is the one described as an unidentified person in our entry on the NCIC."

"Nell, be sure to tell them to hold him and everything found on him or in his car. I will send Max up there to review the inventory and check identification. And call the General and Josh."

Max was briefed and sent on his way. He knew that there was still a lot of mystery remaining unsolved in this case.

19

The Assassin

Max introduced himself to Sgt. Stevens of the Kentucky Highway Patrol: "Sgt., I'm Detective Maxwell. I've been assigned to this case by the Sheriff of Riverside County, Tennessee." Max continued in his usual drawl: "We appreciate your cooperation. What can you tell us?"

"Well, one of our patrol officers was called to the scene of an automobile wreck on a secondary road in McCrackin County. His report does not indicate anything unusual about this one--it was like many others happening on our roads where the driver is under the influence or just gets tired or sleepy and runs off the road, and we then have to clean up the mess. Fortunately he did not run into another vehicle but he broke a utility pole and may have broken his neck too. He died at the scene. Since this happened in our county the coroner may want an autopsy. The body is in the police morgue. It will be released to the family if he has one."

Max asked: "Were you able to identify him?"

"The name on his driver's license is Jacob Anthony Galino. We ran that name through NCIC. The license appears to be have been valid when issued, but it had expired. The name on the driver's license appears to be his real name. This fellow was on parole from his last conviction for racketeering and before that he had a long list of convictions for violent crimes. He is widely known in the underworld of crime as a professional assassin. He earned the name, "The Butcher," because he preferred to kill with a knife instead of a gun which made more noise and usually left ballistic residue for the crime lab. We couldn't miss his missing forefinger. He may have been a victim of some butchery too. He was not the kind of person you would want to have behind your back. You probably have an interest in what we found in his possession."

Sgt. Stevens directed Max's attention to items on a conference room table.

"He was driving a late model Mercedes reported as stolen. A Glock pistol was found in the car, along with a stiletto type knife—not typically a weapon used for self-defense. The serial number on the gun was filed off. He carried a derringer in his pocket. He did not have anything of significance in his billfold— just a pass to a night club in Tunica, Mississippi-- but he did have something of substantial significance in his jacket pocket: Cash—lots of it. He carried it two separate bundles, like you see on the table there."

"Sgt., that is interesting. We may need these items to complete our investigation in Tennessee. I will leave a receipt with you."

Max counted out the currency from each bundle. One bundle contained cash in various amounts in no apparent order—tens, twenties, and fifties--loosely wrapped in a canvas bag like some banks use for handling currency. The other bundle contained cash in fifty dollar bills, neatly arranged and held together with a heavy rubber band. Max counted out one hundred.

Max prepared a receipt and handed it to Sgt. Stevens.

"Sgt., Jacob Anthony Galino may have received justice when he ran off the road. At least he won't have to be extradited and he has saved the State of Tennessee the expense of trying him for murder one."

Max added: "But Tennessee may still have to try a conspirator."

20

The Evidence Room

As Max was placing the items from Kentucky in the evidence room at the crimebusters command center of Riverside County, he thumbed again through the bundle containing the fifty dollar bills. They had been arranged by serial number in consecutive order. An alert light flashed in Max's mind. He used his native reasoning and psychic instinct: "It seems unusual that this bundle contains exactly $5,000 cash. And it is also unusual that the money has been counted out and arranged in consecutive serialized currency. Nobody but a banker would package money like this."

The next stop for Max was the Riverside Bank. He handed the package of fifty dollar currency to Bessie.

"Bessie, I apologize for bothering you again. But have you seen this before?"

"Max, I didn't tell you earlier, but before I handed the money to Clara Cates, I inventoried all of the fifty dollar bills with their serial numbers and kept a list for the bank's records. We did not have to file a Suspicious Activity Report because the amount was under $10,000, but we have an internal policy to keep a record of cash withdrawals to protect the bank against unauthorized withdrawals. Wait here a minute and I will compare the bundled bills with the list."

Bessie came back: "Yes, Max, that is the same money that Clara Cates withdrew in cash."

21

The Arrest of Clara Cates for Criminal Conspiracy

Detective Maxwell was ready to go the District Attorney with his scratch pad. He was followed to the chief prosecutor's office by the Sheriff of Riverside County and the Assistant District Attorney.

The General opened the conference: "I understand that you are prepared to proceed with prosecution in this case. What do you have on Clara Cates? What do you have that I can use in court?"

Max was the spokesperson: "We have the cash which she used to hire her husband's killer."

"That is pretty impressive evidence. How do you know that it is the same money?"

"We traced the fifty dollar bills—serially numbered--from the bank into the hands of Clara Cates. We found the same bills in the hands of the fellow with the missing forefinger. He self destructed in a car wreck. He won't be able to appeal a conviction"

"Detective Max, that is pretty good police work. What else do you have?"

Max thought that should be enough, but added: "She had a motive and had made threats."

The General added: "She also has a motive and the means to hire an expensive defense lawyer. We probably could get a conviction for criminal conspiracy under Section of 39-12-103 of the Code. An overt act is required to carry on a conspiracy to commit a crime, but it is no defense that the object of the conspiracy was not carried through."

Josh offered a comment: "Clara did an overt act when she handed the cash to the contract killer. She may have thought she over paid for the job or wanted a refund, but she didn't back out."

The General continued: "Josh, it usually requires at least two to conspire. When her co-conspirator expired, he could no longer conspire. We may have a problem with the time line. Did Clara Cates deliver the contract money to the contract killer before Henry Cates was robbed and killed for money which he had won at the casino?" Was he killed for the casino money or for the contract money? Max, do you have any notes on this?"

Max pulled out his little pad. "General, there was a date, July 10th, stamped on the bundled cash. We know that Henry was robbed and killed on June 20th. Henry told us in his dying words that he was killed for the casino money, but Clara did not hear this death bed statement. She assumed that the killer had earned the contract money which she had paid him. So, General, it appears that the killer got greedy and collected twice for the same job."

The General deliberated for a moment: "Clara Cates was not cleared or provided an excuse or defense when her contract money was not used. Bring her in and charge her with criminal conspiracy."

22

The Courtroom

The battle lines were forming. The battle ground was the Circuit Court of Riverside County. The battle usually started not by blowing a bugle but by the court officer when he commanded:

"All rise!" and announced: "The Circuit Court of Riverside County is now in session, the Honorable William Bacon presiding. God bless these United States, the State of Tennessee, and this Honorable Court."

The court surely needed divine blessing in trying to find justice in a battle amid the forces of sin and evil. The court officer added a warning to the non-combatants in the courtroom: "There will be no ipads, cell phones, or talking in the courtroom. Whining children will be removed. Do not bring in food, drink, popcorn, chewing tobacco, snuff, or try to get guns, knives, or anything past the detectors that you would not want the Sheriff to see. Disruptive activities will not be allowed. Disruptive dress will be subject to remediation. You do not have to take off your shoes, but take off caps, hats, and hoodies. Do not try to form a cheering or booing section in the courtroom for or against any party."

This warning may not have met all of the constitutional requirements, but it was good enough in the Circuit Court of Riverside County.

The courthouse in Riverside County was a historic structure. The architecture could appropriately be compared to the Roman colosseum where combatants came to fight. Some left with victory. Others were left defeated or mortally wounded on the battleground. The circuit courtroom was built like a theater with a balcony to entertain large crowds which came to town at that time to hear the lawyers try their cases in real life theater. The colorful, flamboyant, trial lawyers with the reputation for persuading a jury with their oratory drew the largest crowds. At that time, the windows served as the only air conditioners and were opened when the lawyers created too much hot air inside. Acoustics was not considered because the lawyers talked loud and long. But the times changed. The crowds came now not to be entertained, but because they had to come for one reason or another.

Judge Bacon sat on the bench in the front middle of the inner courtroom. This was not only an appropriate place for an impartial neutral adjudicator to sit, but it afforded him a broad view of the courtroom and others in the courtroom. The judge's bench was slightly elevated in a cubicle enclosing his chair, desk, computer, books, and necessary equipment. A judges's hammer for keeping law and order was readily available on top of his desk. He had no visible protection against bodily attacks upon himself by deranged or disappointed litigants, but he could take emergency cover inside the cubicle. Other than accepting the existing architecture of the building, there was no rule telling a trial judge how to arrange the courtroom. In Judge Bacon's court, the court reporter sat in the best position to hear; the court clerk sat beside the judge; the court officer sat beside the jury box; the prosecution team sat on the right side of the inside rail facing the judge; the defense team sat on the left side of the inner rail facing the judge; and the prosecution team and the defense team faced each other. And the poor witness sat in his own cubicle box alone, facing the judge, the lawyers, and the jury.

Judge Bacon had practiced law before he was elected Circuit Judge and was known as a lawyer's judge. He had earned a reputation for knowing the law and applying it fairly without bias or prejudice. His trial court opinions were usually affirmed on appeal. He was even tempered with a sense of humor. When his opinion or ruling was faulted by both sides he said that at least he must have got half of it right.

The charge on this battle ground was led by "The General," John Calhoun, the District Attorney General of Riverside County.

23

The Defense Counsel

lonzo Greer defended the other side of the battleground. He was hired by Clara Cates. He sat in the "front chair" of the defense team. Alonzo Greer was widely known around the country as the lawyer to hire in hard cases, and his reputation had preceded him to the country venue of Riverside County. His record for acquittals in defense of wealthy high profile defendants in difficult criminal cases was reported to be measured by, or at least related to, the retainers of six figures or more he was paid by wealthy clients. He said that his job was not to determine guilt or innocence, or the degree of guilt. That was the court's job. He thought that a guilty client was punished enough when he paid the retainer. Alonzo Greer had the reputation of being tenacious, fearless, and intimidating. His expertise in criminal defense was his ability to destroy a witness on cross examination. But his expertise was not limited to cross examination. He also knew the law and how to use it. He did not worry about bringing a brief case to court loaded with books and research notes. His mind was not loaded with irrelevant facts. He was focused. He crafted the defense before trial and tried most cases from notes out of his pocket. He knew before trial what needed to be said and how it should be said. His summations to the jury were dramatic and convincing. Sometimes he was referred to as Lon, the Lion. He could roar like a lion when he wanted to rouse inattentive jurors and then quickly change the tone of his voice, to a near whisper, and crouch closely before the jurors when he wanted to get them up on the edge of their seats.

Alonzo Greer believed in preparation. He subjected his clients to repeated cross examination in the office. He considered these exercises as survival training for the courtroom combat to follow. There would be no time then to exchange signals, wink, or frown. He thought that cosmetics was important, if not too artificial. He wanted his clients to be prepared not only for cross examination and but also for their appearance and demeanor in court. He knew that most jurors paid more attention to demeanor and how a witness looked when testifying than what the witness was saying.

24

The FBI Informant

The combatants were prepared and getting ready for trial. The judge had ruled upon several pretrial motions. The motion to suppress evidence of the dying declaration and the objection to the use of a dead witness, Henry Cates, who could not be confronted in court and cross examined, had become moot with the death of Galino. The case against the co-defendant, Clara Cates, remained set for trial. The General was ready. The Assistant District Attorney General, Josh Wilson, was ready with his research notes. Alonzo, the Lion, was ready to roar. Detective Maxwell, the Possum, was ready with his note pad. A panel of citizens had been summoned who were ready to be trial jurors. The newspaper and television reporters were ready for headline news. The networks had already set up pairs of opposing legal experts and analysts to debate on television the guilt or innocence of Clara Cates, the remaining accused .

While the General was looking over the jury list, he was paged by his secretary: "Mr. Calhoun, you have a call from someone who says he is with the FBI."

"Beth, take the name and number, and I will return the call."

John Calhoun, like most district attorneys in law enforcement, talked freely and frequently with FBI agents about the investigation of crimes, laboratory tests of evidence, and prosecutions in which they had a mutual interest. These exchanges of information were considered routine and usually exchanged in encrypted communication providing both voice security and authentication of the calling party. But this call was from an unknown person over a landline telephone which only provided caller ID. John Calhoun asked himself: "Was this call a prank call from some nut I have convicted? Oh, well, I will return the call."

The General's call was answered at the other end: "Mr. Calhoun, I am an agent with the Federal Bureau of Investigation. I need to talk to you about Jacob Anthony Galino."

"How do I know you are who you say you are?"

"Mr. Calhoun, my call is genuine. I am making this call with the approval and upon the direction of my managers in the Atlanta office, and with knowledge of FBI headquarters in Washington."

"Why do you want to talk to me about Galino?"

"Galino was one of our informants. We want you to protect his identity and keep this call confidential."

The General sat in stunned silence until he was able to speak: "Send me proof of your authority and an explanation why you want me to protect his identity, and I will think about it."

25

The Shield

A highly publicized trial of a high profile defendant represented by an expensive high profile trial attorney might not be considered unusual for Riverside County, but the ghost of a dead FBI informant in the case would be unusual. The General knew that the FBI used informants, like most other law enforcement agencies, but he did not know how FBI informants were recruited and used until the Associated Press reported on an investigation made by aggressive investigative reporters. This exposed a serious flaw in the criminal judicial system:

The government recruited criminals to convict other criminals. This was based upon the theory that a crook knew how to catch a bigger crook; that a thief knew how to catch another thief; that a hacker knew how to catch a smarter hacker; and so on. Informants were recruited to inform on racketeers, gamblers, importers and dealers in illegal drugs, "hit men" and mobsters, including some in the Mafia families. These informants were provided a shield and assured of protection from prosecution. Some were tipped off when other law enforcement agents were closing in. Interrogations were blocked. Some were relocated and given a new identity. One demanded funds for plastic surgery to change his appearance. Some even received written commendations from high level headquarters for doing dirty work. Thinking that this shield gave them an unlimited license to steal, deal, and hit, whenever and wherever they wanted, the recruits turned to profiting from other crime, including murder. This shield of protection allowed them to develop their own "businesses" with a guarantee of exclusive franchises and territories for the commission of crime. This form of immunity was considered better than diplomatic immunity. The "handlers" had lost the handles on the recruits.

Jacob Anthony Galino was one of these maverick informants who had been turned loose and became a professional killer.

So instead of having the satisfaction of bringing to justice, face to face in the courtroom, a killer known as the Butcher, the General was faced with the ghost of a dead confidential FBI informant with the missing forefinger.

26

Trial or Plea?

The prosecution team met in the crime buster's command center to discuss strategy. The chief prosecutor, District Attorney General John Calhoun, presided:

"Men, we have a decision to make, and we have to make it now. You know now about the informant. When he died he received his final, irreversible judgment and cheated us not only out of trying him as a co-conspirator but also made our case against Clara Cates more difficult. He has removed himself from our using him as a witness against her or negotiating a plea with him for his testimony. He has become the ghost of a co-conspirator, and the jury may wonder why he was an informant in the first place."

Josh, the Assistant, opined: "But, General, Clara remains a culpable defendant."

"Yes, Josh, she is culpable, but how culpable?" The General answered his own question: "That is for the jury to decide, and they may have different opinions about the extent of her criminal guilt."

Sheriff Drake entered the discussion: "Well, we all know that Clara Cates was mean and had the motive and desire to do away with Henry, but there are a lot of people running loose out there who in their minds would like to kill somebody they don't like and maybe even form a malicious intent in their minds to do it. Is that a crime?"

The General offered his opinion: "Not as long as the intent is kept inside the mind."

This provided Detective Maxwell an opportunity to offer an opinion: "I guess they could use psychic voo doo and stick pins in a model of anyone they want to be rid of."

The General continued: "Of course, Clara formed a criminal intent in her mind and she did not keep it in her mind. I find it rather ironic that Henry's dying declaration unintentionally provided her with some defense cover when he said that he was killed for the gambling money."

The Sheriff returned to the discussion: "If Henry was killed for the gambling money, and not for Clara's contract money, where does that leave Clara?"

Josh answered: "She lost her contract money. She should have been left with a bad conscience, but that may not be enough for her to express remorse and plead guilty to any crime. She could claim that she was punished enough when she paid her expensive defense lawyer."

The Sheriff added: "Consider too that this woman does not have a criminal record of any kind that can be used against her. She can show that she still has three children to educate in college, and that she can continue to be a productive citizen in the community."

The General agreed: "And if she goes to trial she will not have to testify against herself."

The General concluded the discussion: "We are ready to try this case, but it may also be a case in which to consider a plea."

Epilogue

The District Attorney General and Clara Cates's attorney negotiated a plea, which was approved by the Judge, allowing her to plead guilty to an attempt to commit a conspiracy. She was sentenced to three years to be served in the Riverside County jail. The sentence was suspended subject to her completion of community service, including working personally under direct supervision of a probation officer building two homes for Habitat for Humanity. Thus, the file on the case of the felon with the missing forefinger was closed. The Sheriff of Riverside County was ready for the next call. The District Attorney was ready for the next case, and Detective Maxwell, the possum, was ready for his next assignment.

About the Author

Allen Shoffner is a graduate of Vanderbilt University School of Law, where he was a member of, and authored legal articles for, the Vanderbilt Law Review. He has authored various articles in legal publications and served six years on the Tennessee Law Revision Commission. In 2001 he researched, authored, and published a historical novel, *The Authority*, about the misuse and abuse of governmental power by the Tennessee Valley Authority. In 2007 he wrote and published *In Sickness and In Health, A Love Story*, a true story about tests of faith in struggling with the long-term illness of his wife. In 2008 he wrote and published *A Bicentennial History of Shofner's Lutheran Church*, the historic church on the waters of Thompson Creek in Bedford County, Tennessee. In 2011 he wrote and published *Collectanea*, a collection of his unpublished writings. In 2012 he wrote and published *The Adventures of a Tennessee Farm Boy, A Journey From the Farm to the Courtroom*. Allen Shoffner was active in trial and appellate practice of law for over fifty-six years.